....

....

LEABHARLANN CHONTAE NA MIDHE

SEIRBHÍS SCOILE

Ginn is a registered trademark of Harcourt Education Ltd

Linacre House, Jordan Hill, Oxford, OX2 8DP
a division of Harcourt Education Ltd

**Visit www.myprimary.co.uk to see a chart showing you all the
Pocket Reads programme information you will need.**

Alien Encounter © Robert Hood 2000

From the Spinouts project developed by Paul Collins and Meredith Costain.

08 07 06
10 9 8 7 6 5 4 3 2
ISBN 0 602 24275 4 / 978 0 602242 75 6

Illustrated by Terry Denton and Phil Garner
Cover illustration by Marc McBride
Designed by Carolyn Gibson
Repro by Digital Imaging, Glasgow
Printed and bound in China through Phoenix Offset

Robert Hood

Robert Hood writes strange stories about strange things. Some people say that this is because he is very strange himself. However, just because he talks to the rubber monster on top of his computer and wears vampire fangs to work doesn't mean he's unusual, does it?

About the story

"I found myself wondering what it might be like to have a little friend only you could hear, who came on a surprise visit."

Robert Hood

CHAPTER 1

A Tickle in the Brain

Max could *feel* the voice inside his head. It was almost like something tickling the edges of his brain. He couldn't catch the actual words, but he knew it was a voice. It was a loud voice, but it came from a long way off. It made him dizzy.

– *Zyert-folipp-oob!* it said.

Max knew there was only one explanation. He must be really ill. Maybe he was dying!

"Mum!" he yelled, running into the sitting room. "I'm sick."

"Sick?" She looked worried. His father looked up, but said nothing. "What's wrong?" asked Mum.

"I feel dizzy," said Max.

"Dizzy?" said Mum.

"I'm hearing things."

"Hearing things?"

"There's noises in my head."

"Noises in your head?"

"And I keep hearing everything I say twice, like an echo," said Max.

"Oh, very funny," said Mum crossly. "Don't be a smarty-pants, Maxwell. Go to bed."

"Honest. I'm sick." Max grabbed Mum's hand and put it against his forehead. "Have I got a temperature?"

"No. Just go to bed, Max," said Mum firmly.

"But –"

His father stirred. "You heard your mother. Bed!"

Max trudged back to his room, feeling his forehead. It wasn't fair. They never took any notice of him. But his mum was right. He didn't have a temperature. So why was he hearing voices?

CHAPTER 2

Lizardguts

Sometime after midnight Max fell asleep, worn out from searching through the rubbish in his room. No one was hiding in the cupboard. There were no hidden microphones anywhere. Nothing.

But early next morning, when he woke up, he heard the voice again, deep in his head. – *Zyert-folipp-oob!*

"What's that supposed to mean?" said Max crossly. He was getting fed up with the voice. He dug in his ear with his finger, but there was nothing there except wax.

The voice became clearer. – *It means "if you can't hear me, stick your finger in your ear".*

"You're kidding!" said Max.

– *No, I'm not. Sticking your finger in your ear makes a small change in your brain. That's why you can understand me clearly now.*

"Really? Who are you?"

– *My name's Lizardguts.*

A silly name, Max thought, but he decided not to say anything about it. At least not until he found out whether or not he was going crazy.

"Where are you from?" Max asked.

– *The planet Molebelly in the Gargellian Nebula, which is 1234 billion zarbelwags from the Great Blirt. Do you know it?*

"Never heard of it."

– *What about you? Where are you from?*

Right now, Max wasn't even sure what day it was. "I'm from the planet Earth," he said. "I haven't got the foggiest idea where it is, though."

– *Hmm,* said the voice.

"But how come I can hear you?" said Max. "How come you know how to speak English?"

– *Ah! Now, that's very interesting. I'm broadcasting through a wormhole using Weez Operator technology. But it's very rare that we can focus in on someone as far away as you. Let me explain ...*

"It's OK," said Max quickly. "What are you like, then?"

– *Like?*

"Yeah. Describe yourself."

The voice seemed to think for a moment. – *Well, I'm pretty small, I guess, and I'm green.*

"Wow!" gasped Max. "You're a little green man from outer space. Just like everyone talks about."

– Little and green, yes. I don't know about 'man' though.

"Well, I'm BIG," Max boasted. "I'm even taller than my dad." Then he paused. "He's a squirt – like you!"

The voice didn't say anything. Max wondered if he had gone too far. Maybe Lizardguts didn't like being teased about his height. "Being small's OK, though," Max added. "I was small once, but I've grown up. Have you grown up?"

– What does 'grown up' mean?

"Well," explained Max, feeling very clever. "Humans start out as babies, who are sort of small and soggy, then they turn into kids, who are bigger and can talk and play video games, and after that they grow into adults, who are really big and drive cars."

– *Oh, my!* Lizardguts sounded impressed. – *That sounds very weird.*

Lizardguts and Max talked for ages, until Max's mum came in ranting and raving about him being late for school.

"Maybe you're sick after all," his mum said. "You're muttering to yourself."

"Nah," said Max. "I'm big and important and not a bit sick!"

Mum scowled at him, so he went and got ready for school.

CHAPTER 3

Good News, Very Big Max!

Lizardguts was quiet for the rest of the day.
From time to time, when he thought no one
was listening, Max would yell, "Hey, Gutsy,
are you there?" or "Speak up, Lizardbreath,
I can't hear you!" But there was no reply.

Several times other kids and his teachers caught him talking to nobody. From the looks on their faces, they obviously thought he'd gone bananas. He made rude faces at them. They thought they were *sooo* smart, but they didn't have a clue. He was the one with a friend from outer space.

But where had his friend got to?

Lizardguts popped into his head again just as Max was drifting off to sleep that night.

– *Good news, Very Big Max!*

"Where have you been all day, Gutsy?" said Max.

– *I've been speaking to the leader of Molebelly, President Dogsbreath.*

Max laughed so much he nearly choked. "Your president's name is Dogsbreath?"

*– Yes indeed. He is very important. I
asked for Special Permission. And I got it!*

"Special permission? To do what?"

*– Visit you! I like you, Very Big Max.
You're my friend. I want to speak to you
face-to-face.*

"All right!" cried Max. "That'd be great. I
can't wait to see the teacher's face when I
bring you to Show and Tell. But Gutsy," he

said. "You're zillions of whatsits away. I'll be dead by the time you get here, won't I?"

– *I know what you're thinking,* said Lizardguts. *But you're forgetting about the Wombat-tooth Theory.*

"As discovered by Professor Wombat-tooth, right?"

– *Yes. How did you know about him?*

"Lucky guess."

– *The Wombat-tooth Theory showed that …*

"Stop!" cried Max. Don't bother to tell me. You'll frazzle my brain. Basically what you're saying is, you'll be here soon!"

– *Yes indeed.*

"Well, how soon?"

– *Oh,* said Lizardguts. – *How about tomorrow morning?*

CHAPTER 4

The Little Guy

Max was so excited he could hardly sleep. Lizardguts, a little green thingy from outer space, was coming to Earth to visit *him*. Max. Not the Prime Minister. Not the President of the United States. But *him*.

He hoped Lizardguts was big enough to be really impressive on TV.

When he woke in the morning, Max listened to see if Lizardguts had left any messages. Nothing. So he lay in bed staring at the ceiling.

An hour later there was a tickle at the edge of his brain.

"Lizardguts?" he said.

– Hi, Very Big Max. I'm here! Lizardguts' voice sounded much louder. It boomed in Max's head.

"Really?" Max sat up fast. He looked around the room but couldn't see anything strange. "Where are you?"

– I'm on a huge flat plain. It's sort of crunchy underfoot and there's swarms of ants running around ...

"There's no plains around here," said Max. "This is the suburbs. Lots of houses and stuff." Max heard a deep rumbling noise and his room shook. "And there's a thunderstorm coming. Is there a thunderstorm where you are?"

– No, the weather's fine.

"Well, you must have got lost."

– Impossible. I know I'm near you somewhere. I just can't see you.

Max sighed. Lizardguts was probably on a different planet altogether. "Oh well," Max said. "I'll have a look around and see if I can see you, little guy."

Thunder shook the room again. There was a bad storm coming.

Max put on a sweatshirt, and went down to the front door. His parents weren't around. It was Saturday morning, so they'd probably gone shopping.

Max opened the door. Thunder boomed.

The first thing Max thought was: *It's not thunder. It's footsteps.*

There were two gigantic feet out there, each one bigger than King Kong. They were so big they crushed dozens of houses with each step. People were screaming and running around like ants.

Max looked up at the legs attached to the feet, then up further at the monstrous green body attached to the legs and – way, way up – at the massive head.

The ground shook and split apart.

The second – and last – thing Max thought was: *If Lizardguts is just a little guy, how big must the others be?*